COLORING ABOUT CHRISTMAS

Pictures and Rhymes
By Emma C. McKean

WITH UNDERLINED WORDS IN RHYME

CATHOLIC BOOK PUBLISHING CORP.
New Jersey

Singing Christmas carols,
Is a joyful thing to <u>do</u>.
Not only right at Christmas
time,
But through the New Year, <u>too</u>.

(T-680)

© 1986 Catholic Book Publishing Corp., N.J.

Printed in China

2 ISBN 978-0-89942-680-8 CPSIA May 2014 10 9 8 7 6 5 4 3 2 1 K/Y

NIHIL OBSTAT: Daniel V. Flynn, J.C.D., *Censor Librorum*
IMPRIMATUR: Joseph T. O'Keefe, D.D.
Vicar General, Archdiocese of New York
www.catholicbookpublishing.com

JOY to the WORLD

MERRY CHRISTMAS

PEACE ON EARTH

Christmas is the Birthday
of JESUS.
Believe! Appreciate!
He came to be Our SAVIOR.
How wonderful! How great!

Christmas is so special.
May all believers know.
Our HEAVENLY FATHER
sent HIS SON,
Because HE loves us so.

The NEW TESTAMENT
begins with the Gospel of Matthew.

EMMANUEL
means
"God is with us."

Matthew, in the words
used by Isaiah,
Tells how JESUS, OUR SAVIOR,
came;—

Born of the VIRGIN MARY,
with the Messiah's
meaningful NAME!

Virgin Mary
and Child Jesus

MARY,
Mother of JESUS

The Angel Gabriel told Mary
when the HOLY SPIRIT would
come over her, that <u>SHE</u>
Would become the
Blessed Virgin,
MOTHER of JESUS.
The SON OF GOD IS <u>HE</u>.

WHEN JESUS WAS BORN

Shepherds watching sheep,
Keeping them in <u>sight</u>,
Heard a shining angel bring
Wondrous news to <u>light</u>,

About the newborn Savior,
Who in a manger <u>lay</u>,
In Bethlehem's city of David
Not very far <u>away</u>.

WHERE JESUS WAS BORN

Many angels appeared and
were singing,
The wonderful hymn of <u>joy</u>,

As the shepherds saw,
The Son of God,
The Infant Savior <u>Boy</u>.

12

Jesus was born in BETHLEHEM.

When JESUS was presented
in the Temple,
About forty days after HIS <u>birth</u>,
The priest who was privileged to
greet HIM,
Knew the reason
HE came
to this <u>earth</u>.

The Blessed Virgin Mary presented
JESUS in the TEMPLE

Our HEAVENLY FATHER
sent JESUS,
To save us and
show us the <u>WAY</u>,
To live through
faith,
and hope,
and love,
Forever, and <u>today</u>.

We rejoice with praise
and thanksgiving,
As we kneel down to <u>adore</u>,
The SPIRITUAL GIFT of OUR SAVIOR,
As the shepherds did, <u>before</u>.

DIVINE PRAISES

Blessed be God.
Blessed be His Holy Name.

Blessed be Jesus Christ,
true God and true Man.

Blessed be the Name
of Jesus.

Samuel is
thinking about,
The Wise Men who
traveled from <u>afar</u>,

To find the promised
SAVIOR KING,
By following
the <u>STAR</u>!

21

THE THREE WISE MEN

When the Wise Men
came from the
East to <u>behold</u>,

The NEWBORN KING
They brought presents
with <u>gold</u>.

24

When the Wise Men left,
to return no <u>more</u>,
'twas by a different route than they
traveled <u>before</u>.

<u>Two Christmas Dotographs</u>
Draw straight lines
from dot 1 to 11, to <u>see</u>

Two Christmas
pictures
— a star
and a <u>tree</u>.

5 •

4 •

3 •

6 •

7 •

2 •

8 •

•1

•10

•11

•9

26

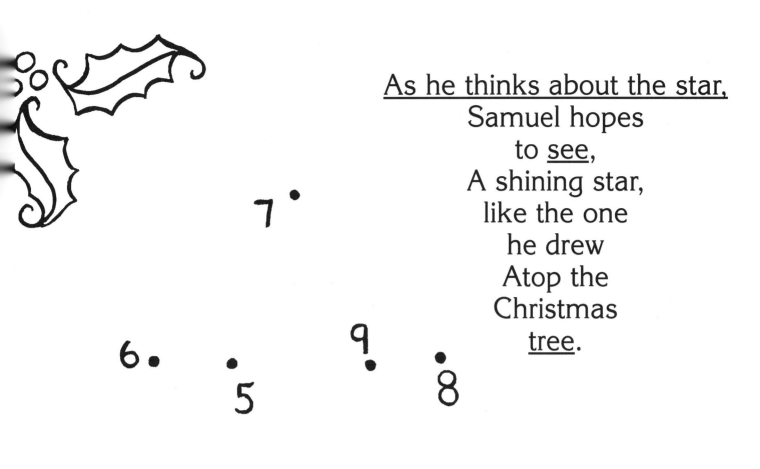

As he thinks about the star,
Samuel hopes
to see,
A shining star,
like the one
he drew
Atop the
Christmas
tree.

7

6 5

9 8

4 3

10 11

1

2

KEEP
CHRIST
IN
CHRISTMAS

THE CHRISTMAS POSTER

When Andrew made a poster,
Eileen put it on the <u>wall</u>,
Where everyone could see it—
People big,
    or <u>small</u>.

These children made
    a Christmas card,
A very special one—
    A loving "Thank You
    Birthday card,"
For JESUS CHRIST,
GOD'S SON.

Upon the birthday of OUR LORD,
    Joanne and Stephen pray,
    That we may all appreciate
OUR SAVIOR'S love today.

THANK YOU, JESUS

Thanks be to GOD
For the GOOD NEWS—
THE <u>WAY</u>—
Our SAVIOR came to earth
for us,
Christmas <u>DAY</u>.